Mouse and the Storm

CHILDREN'S REFLEXOLOGY TO REDUCE ANXIETY AND HELP SOOTHE THE SENSES

SUSAN QUAYLE

ILLUSTRATED BY MELISSA MULDOON

SINGING DRAGON

LONDON AND PHILADELPHIA

First published in 2017
by Singing Dragon
an imprint of Jessica Kingsley Publishers
73 Collier Street
London N1 9BE, UK and
400 Market Street, Suite 400
Philadelphia, PA 19106, USA

www.singingdragon.com

Library of Congress Cataloging in Publication Data
A CIP catalog record for this book is available from the Library of Congress

British Library Cataloguing in Publication Data
A CIP catalogue record for this book is available from the British Library

ISBN 978 1 84819 344 4
eISBN 978 0 85701 300 2

Printed and bound in China

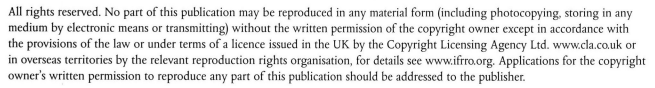

For Jack and his mum, Tracy, with thanks.

Foreword

As a parent you strive to support your child to be independent and happy in their lives; when you have a child with additional needs the journey to achieve this can be sometimes challenging and diverse. Using reflexology with our son has enabled us to have some quiet, calm and positive time together in what can sometimes be a challenging and busy day. This beautiful story is both engaging and interactive and guides you through the reflex points to support your child's own needs.

As a family we have enjoyed sharing the story and taking the time to use the reflexology both as parent to child but also supporting our son to learn to use the specific reflex points to enable him to help himself when he is feeling anxious or overwhelmed. He will often ask for his 'hand massage' when we are in busy places or at bedtime to help calm and relax him ready for sleep.

We have very much enjoyed being able to use this book as part of our journey in supporting our son to increase his independence and autonomy. We hope you do too!

Tracy Weiner, Chair at Phoenix Autism Centre,
Tonbridge and mother of Jack

Contents

Introduction

The Children's Reflexology Programme has been designed to enable parents, carers, family and friends to offer children the benefits of Reflexology in a way that is fun, relaxing and supports natural bonding.

This book is intended to extend our programme to include children with additional needs. I have created a story that focuses on the disruption of change and how important it can be for things to get back to a sense of normality. This can be helpful for children who have Autism, children who don't cope well with new experiences, children who suffer from high anxiety and many other conditions and situations that children increasingly find themselves in these days.

I have used reflexology of the hands in this book as this treatment gives children with complex needs the chance to get up and walk away, should they need to, as well as being able to perform the reflexology on themselves. This is extremely important to many children as it offers them self-empowerment and a strategy to be able to manage their emotional control as well as other elements of their conditon.

It is also very helpful for children who suffer from Sensory Processing Dysfunction as they can regulate their own touch with this programme. Children who have used the book have already found a connection between the animal characters and their own hands, finding it useful to visit them throughout the day at times of anxiety and transition.

Reflexology is a gentle, non-invasive Complementary Therapy that can help with many common ailments of childhood. The hands contain reflex points that correspond to different parts of the body. When these reflexes are manipulated it helps to ease problems within that area of the body as well as supporting the body's own ability to self-heal.

As well as offering invaluable therapeutic benefits, this book is designed to aid in the bonding process between the adult and the child. Time spent reading these stories at bedtime and performing the actions on the child will create a sense of quality time, fun and positive touch between you. The time you spend in a positive way relating these stories

will offer help, distraction, comfort and a feeling of safety at other times in your child's life. In my experience children can be brought back from utter distress with a comforting distraction that is familiar to them.

It is also a way for parents and carers to offer help at times when they feel helpless. This book offers parents of children with additional needs a connection with their child that they may not have had before. This programme is already bringing families together, with the child giving parents and siblings the reflexology from the book.

Repeated regularly, these stories can help to support your child's good health. They can also offer the parent the chance to catch a problem before it develops and becomes out of control.

Conditions such as constipation and colic can be relieved before they become a problem through regular treatments. Reflexology can also be used to work alongside conventional medicine to support more serious conditions such as asthma and epilepsy. As a Complementary Therapist I would never encourage anyone to stop taking prescribed medication unless it had been sanctioned by their doctor.

The Gentle Touch

When working on very young children – newborns, babies and toddlers – it is essential that you use a very light touch. Children's bones and musculature will be undeveloped and their reflexes may be very sensitive. It is unlikely that you will hurt your child, unless you use a very strong pressure, but it will not be conducive to the relaxing and positive results we are after.

Older children with conditions such as Cerebral Palsy may require attentive positioning before reflexology as it can have a particularly relaxing effect upon muscles.

Never perform reflexology on a child if you are feeling angry, as it is important that the experience remains a positive one for everyone, especially them.

Basic Reflexology Techniques

Caterpillar

The caterpillar, or thumb and finger walking, will be the most-used technique. You literally move your finger or thumb up and down the reflex in a caterpillar motion – bending the finger or thumb and then straightening as you move forward and then repeating.

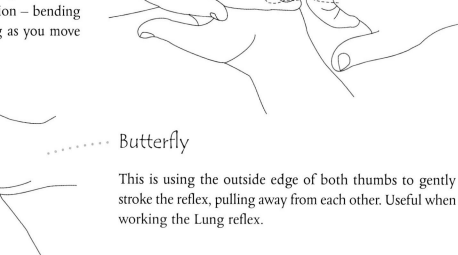

Butterfly

This is using the outside edge of both thumbs to gently stroke the reflex, pulling away from each other. Useful when working the Lung reflex.

Finger Stroking

This is basically what it says. Use a gentle motion with a light pressure.

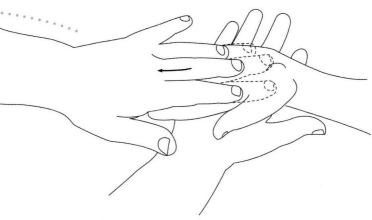

Hand Stroking

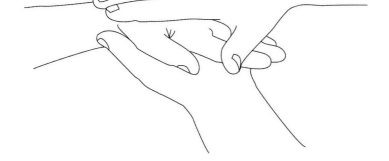

Gently glide your hands, palms down, over the child's hands, completely enveloping them with the warmth and comfort of your hands. Glide the hand up toward the arm and then down the sides before starting over. Very relaxing, and a lovely way to begin and end the story.

The Story and How to Use This Book

This story is based around a group of animal characters. The intention is that each animal represents a particular reflex area. For example, the central character is a mouse. She represents the Solar plexus, which is very important in all conditions related to pain, discomfort, stress and anxiety. Mouse appears in all the stories and you will return to her reflex regularly to help your child feel calm.

Each page of the story has a diagram of the hands in the corner showing the reflexes that you should be working, with written instructions on what to do. This story will provide a general reflexology treatment for your child. This means that the main reflexes will be manipulated if you follow the instructions alongside the hand maps on each page.

This story is based on the effects of an unexpected event and the resolution of these events. It is intended to reflect any everyday disruption and to remind us that they can always be resolved.

The Reflexes and Characters

The characters in these books each represent a reflex area of the hand. As you visit each of the reflexes, the character representing that reflex appears in the story.

Here are the characters you will meet.

Mouse

Mouse represents the Solar Plexus reflex point. She is the central character and you will return to her again and again.

Squirrel

Squirrel represents the Head, Sinus, Teeth, Eyes and Ear reflexes.

Hare

Hare represents the Lungs and Chest reflexes.

Mole

Mole represents the Digestive System reflexes.

Otter

Otter represents the Lymphatic System reflex.

Snake

Snake represents the Nervous System, Back and Spine reflexes.

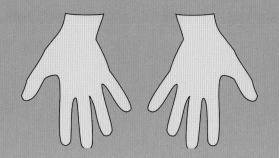

Gently stroke your child's hands to prepare them for their Reflexology treatment.

In the ocean blue and deep
Sat an island chain that looked like feet
Toward its shores a big storm blew
And no one on the island knew

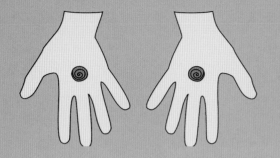

Hold your child's hands in your hands with your thumb gently pressed on the Solar Plexus reflex.

Mouse was curled up in her nest
Her favourite place that she liked best
The sky was cloudy, looking grey
An early night for her today

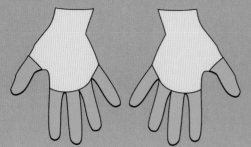

Gently caterpillar walk up the fingers on the palm side of the hand.

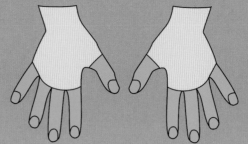

Gently caterpillar walk down the fingers on the top of the hand.

Gently circle the tops of the fingers.

Squirrel slept soundly in his tree
On a bed of fresh beech leaves
He'd worked so hard to make his bed
He was snoring before leaves touched his head

 16

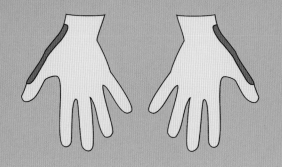

Gently caterpillar walk down the outside of the side of the thumb.

Slowly work your way back using tiny gentle circular movements.

Snake was cosy on his rock
In his bed of herbs and hops
Without the heat from the sun
Hide and seek was just no fun

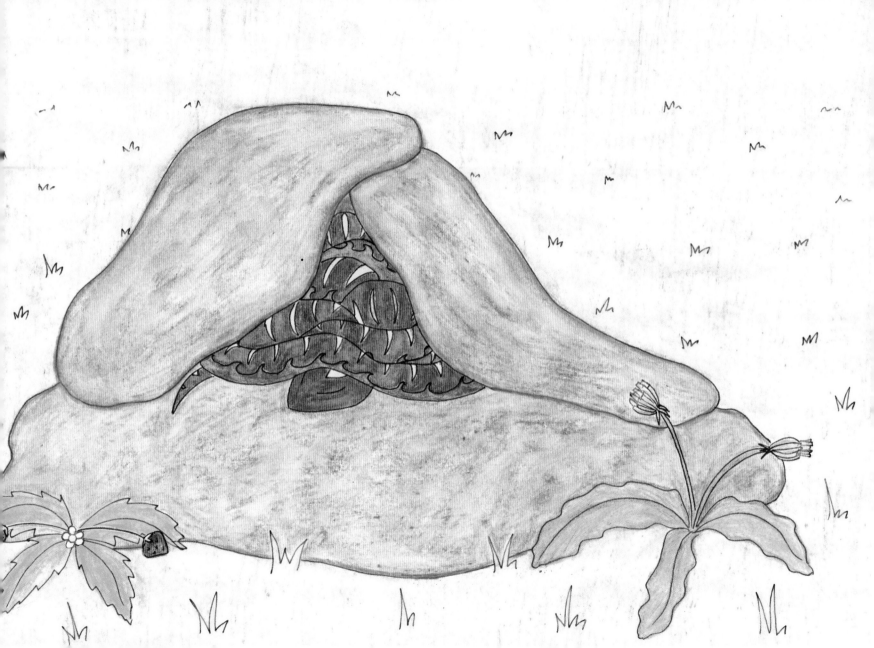

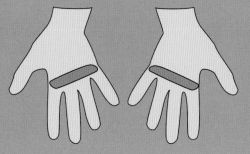

Gently caterpillar walk, or butterfly stroke, below the fingers at the top of the palm of the hand.

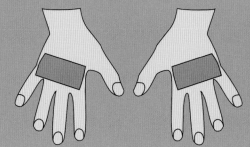

Gently caterpillar walk down the top of the hand, from the base of the fingers down the metacarpals and in between.

Hare was curled up in the grass
On the open plain, wide and vast
He'd run so fast throughout the day
He fell fast asleep in his bed of hay

Begin on the top of the thumbs, caterpillar walk
down them both then follow the numbers.

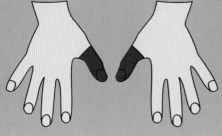

1. Gently slide your thumb
down following the number 1.

2. Starting on the right
hand, slide your thumb
across from right to left.

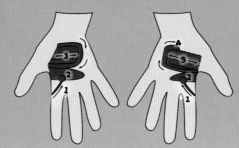

3. Caterpillar walk to and
fro to follow number 3.

4. Starting on the right hand,
gently caterpillar walk to
follow the horseshoe.

With crystal stars above his head
Mole softly snored upon his bed
He often slept, morning, noon or night
His bedroom didn't have a light

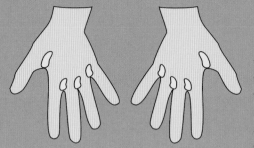

Caterpillar walk from the base of the fingers down the top of the hand. Butterfly stroke the top of the hand.

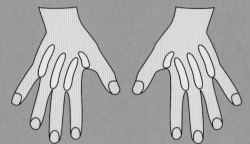

Gently using tiny circles work your way around the top of the wrist, gently stroking up the arm.

Otter dreamt on his eider down bed
Shoals of silver fish filled his head
He chased them down through the watery deep
His body twitching in his sleep

Gently press your fist into the palm of your child's hand. Move down the hand with each press.

Out in the ocean the waves grew steep
And crashed all foaming and white on the beach
The wind was a funnel that blew round and round
Picking things up and putting them down

Using the palms of your hands create small circles down the sides of each hand, like a locomotive.

All the animals were still asleep
Not one of them made a single peep
The howling wind swept through the land
The giant waves crashed on the sand

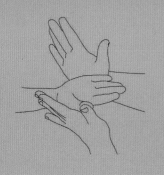

Slide the flat palm of your
hands up and down the sides
of your child's hands.

In the morning the sky was blue
The golden sun arose anew
Mouse woke up and looked around
She was in a tree high off the ground

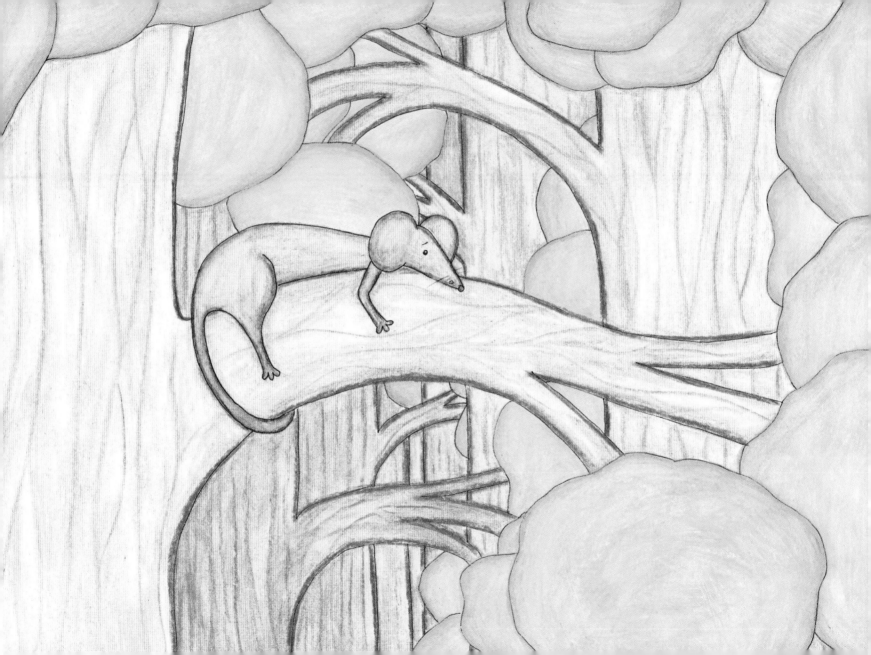

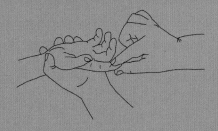

Gently turn each finger in one direction and then reverse in the opposite direction.

Squirrel woke to Mole's bedroom light
Stars in the rock roof shiny and bright

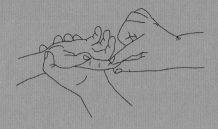

Gently pull each finger.

Snake woke up cold and a little bit damp
In Otter's Holt feeling terribly cramped

Create small butterfly strokes
down the palm and on top
of your child's hand.

Hare was half cold but smelt lavender sweet
Mouse's house was too small for his legs and his feet

Create a raindrop effect using the pads of your fingertips to gently tap your child's palms.

Mole was too hot and the light was too bright
How did he get to Snake's house last night?

Create a raindrop effect using the tops of your fingers to gently tap beneath your child's hands.

Otter had woken on the high grassy plain
He was desperate to get back to the water again

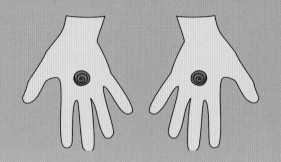

Hold your child's hand in your hands with your thumb gently pressed on the Solar Plexus reflex.

The animals were feeling frightened and strange
They wanted to go home; to feel normal again
Mouse thought of her nest with her eyes closed tight
And climbed down the tree quivering with fright

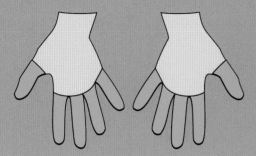

Gently caterpillar walk up the fingers on the palm side of the hand.

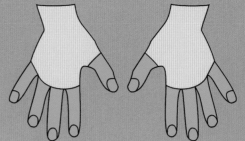

Gently caterpillar walk down the fingers on the top of the hand.

Gently circle the tops of the fingers.

Then she went to Mole's house and set Squirrel free
And took him back to his comfortable tree
Settled him down in fresh green leaves
With a bag of nuts and a cup of mint tea

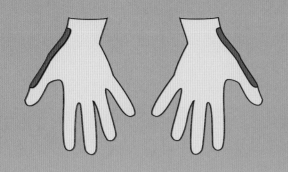

Gently caterpillar walk down the outside of the side of the thumb.

Slowly work your way back using tiny gentle circular movements.

She rescued poor Snake from the cold and the cramp
Got him back in the sun and out of the damp
His rock was warm from the hot morning sun
But he wasn't quite ready to start having fun

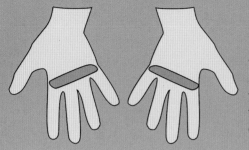

Gently caterpillar walk, or butterfly stroke, below the fingers at the top of the palm of the hand.

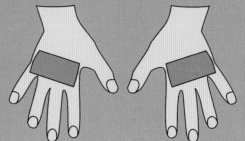

Gently caterpillar walk down the top of the hand, from the base of the fingers down the metacarpals and in between.

Hare had run fast back up to the plain
To get his poor legs working again
Once he started he just couldn't stop
A leap and a jump a kick and a hop

Begin on the top of the thumbs, caterpillar walk
down them both then follow the numbers.

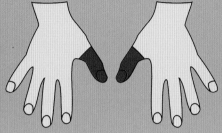

1. Gently slide your thumb
down following the number 1.

2. Starting on the right
hand, slide your thumb
across from right to left.

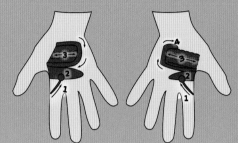

3. Caterpillar walk to and
fro to follow number 3.

4. Starting on the right hand,
gently caterpillar walk to
follow the horseshoe.

Mouse took Mole to a mound in the floor
Where a cool, dark tunnel led to his front door
Mole laughed with joy when he reached the shade
And Mouse shook off the mess he'd made

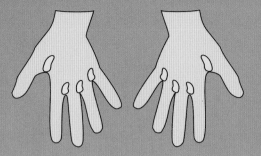

Caterpillar walk from the base of the fingers down the top of the hand. Butterfly stroke the top of the hand.

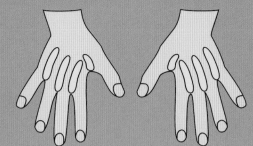

Gently using tiny circles work your way around the top of the wrist, gently stroking up the arm.

Then she walked with Otter back down to the sea
And laughed as she watched him jump in and swim free
The sun shining down on his bubbling trail
As down he dived like a humpback whale

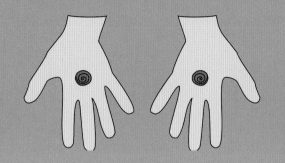

Hold your child's hand, in your hands with your thumb gently pressed on the Solar Plexus reflex.

Then she set off for home, to her own cosy nest
For what, she considered, a well-deserved rest
Squirrel was waiting with berries and tea
And a question: 'How did you climb down from that tree?'

The Children's Reflexology Programme

The Children's Reflexology Programme for Additional Needs (TCRPAN) has been created to support both parents of and children with additional needs.

Developed alongside TCRP, our plan has always been to reach as many children and their parents as we can with our message on the empowering benefits of reflexology as a gentle, non-invasive complementary therapy.

Run in the same way as our original course, we offer courses for parents to come along and learn our programme in weekly classes that encourage community interaction and support. All our instructors are qualified in TCRPAN and insured. We also offer Instructor training to anyone who has a healthy interest in working with and supporting families with children who have additional needs.

As a way of of creating continuity of care and to support the familes that work with us and our programme, we have also developed a course for carers, and for health care workers and teachers who work with these children on a daily basis.

If you would like to run your own ethical business supporting parents by sharing these gentle techniques please do get in touch.

If you are a carer, care provider, school, special educational needs school or Hospice who would like to bring our programme into your setting please do get in touch, we are happy to discuss your needs.

Whoever you are and whatever your reasons this is a lovely way to bring people together, to support parents with young children and to connect with your own communities.

To find out more about TCRP please visit our website at www.kidsreflex.co.uk.